ALGOMA GHOST:

THE LEGEND OF HELL'S BRIDGE

RUSSELL SLATER

Copyright © 2015 Russell Slater

Edited by Sam Mills

Cover art and design by Laura Gordon
(www.thebookcovermachine.com)

Hangman symbol by Jordan Richardson

All rights reserved.

ISBN: 0692555617
ISBN-13: 978-0692555613

Peninsulam Publishing

Publishing stories Made in Michigan
www.peninsulampublishing.com

Printed in the USA

CONTENTS

Thank you to my family and friends, for your support and encouragement. You are my inspiration.

I would also like to thank Laura Gordon, amazing cover artist, Jordan Richardson, for your awesome hangman symbol design, Sam Mills, editor extraordinaire, Peter Welmerink, my West Michigan writing brother, for your assistance, and my good friend Trevor Williams, for giving me the idea.

PROLOGUE

Laphamville, Michigan
(future site of Rockford)
October 25, 1835

Fear. Anxiety. Urgency.

Two weeks ago, three area children vanished. There was no ready explanation for the disappearance of the two boys, ages five and ten, and a twelve year old girl.

"Fair people of Laphamville, heed my warning!" The log cabin church overflowed with congregants. An imposing figure stood, Bible in hand, before the hand-wringing congregation. Despite his hunched back and stooped shoulders, the man stood an impressive six feet, three inches. His height, white Moses-like beard, deeply set eyes, and thunderous voice leant to the man's air of authority. When Elias Friske spoke, others listened.

"Lucifer is in our midst! He seeks to turn this town away from God's glory! He seeks your eternal souls!" Parishioners gasped, wringing their hands harder.

In a thick Germanic accent, Elias read, "Deuteronomy 18:10-14, 'There shall not be found among you any one that maketh his son or his daughter to pass through the fire, or that useth divination, or an observer of times, or an enchanter, or a witch, or a charmer, or a consulter with familiar spirits, or a wizard, or a necromancer... for all that do these things are an abomination unto the LORD!! And because of these abominations the LORD, your God, is driving them *out* before you.'

Brothers and sisters: Join me in prayer..."

The townspeople lowered their eyes, following the lead of the righteous Elias. The prayer ended with a resounding "AMEN" from all present, and Elias called for a private consultation with the male heads of each household.

Three of the men who met with Elias, their eyes wet from weeping, were the distraught fathers of the missing children. Elias pressed the men to recruit wives and older children for a search party. His urgency mirrored the men's desire to take action.

"Time is of the essence! Dispatch to the woods - post haste!"

\#

FIVE HOURS LATER

The parents of Laphamville's children were exhausted, physically and emotionally. Over densely-wooded hills, across swift-moving streams, and through tepid swamps they searched. It was all in vain. With wet feet, and sweat-soaked clothing, they returned, heads hung in despair and disappointment.

Their throats parched, they stopped near the communal well in the center of town. Ladlefuls of cool water quenched and refreshed, but water did nothing for their sagging spirits.

"We have failed..." uttered one dejected man, the father of the missing girl. "Emily... Phineas... Caleb... we've failed them all." He lowered his head and wept.

"What has the Devil done with my baby?!" The man's obese wife dripped with perspiration, her beet-red cheeks trembling with rage. "*WHERE IS MY EMILY?!*" Her meaty fists slammed into her thighs, emphasizing each word with a downward strike.

The mother of Caleb asked through tears, "Now what do we do?"

Silence. The father of Emily spoke, "Let us seek the guidance of Elias."

"To the church!" shouted the parents.

They arrived at their house of worship, surprised to find it vacant.

"Where is Elias? And the children...?" asked the father of Emily, palms up in question.

At the urging of Friske, the children of Laphamville had been left in his care while the others searched. This righteous, intimidating man was a trusted village elder - a well-known man of God... *wasn't he?*

"Yes, where are the children?" The question fell on silent stares. "What did he do with them??"

\#

Deep in the woodland, near the rushing waters of the River Rogue, they found Elias. Alone. Countenance twisted, huddled at the base of an oak tree, his hands, clothes, and mouth were caked with blood.

"The demons..." he sobbed. "The demons... took them..."

"What are you speaking of, Elias?" demanded mother of Caleb. "Speak clearly!"

Father of Emily seized the man by his crimson-speckled collar, pulling him to his feet. "Where are they, Elias?!" The father shook the big man like a rag doll. *"Where?!?"*

Friske raised his eyes and motioned toward the river.
Emily's father pushed the once-trusted elder in the same
direction, and growled between gritted teeth, "Show us!"

Dazed, Elias stumbled along, leading the villagers
toward the riverbank. A trembling, bony white finger pointed
the way. "There..."

A woman's scream pierced the air. Men gasped and
cursed under their breath. Before them was a vision of
unspeakable horror.

Dozens of little bodies bobbed in the water, a hemp
rope around their waists binding the children in a cluster.
The rope caught on a twisted tree root jutting into the
current, stopping their downstream drift. A morbid flotilla of
death.

Limbs bent at odd angles, broken bones protruding
through skin. Deep cuts across their throats, blood trickling
into the river.

"Retrieve the rope," Emily's father instructed an older
teenage boy.

The boy, shaking, choked, "Why...?"

"This bastard's gonna hang. An eye for an eye! Retrieve
the rope..."

The boy complied while the other villagers carried their

deceased offspring out of the river, carefully laying them in rows on the grass.

Father of Emily tied the rope in a noose while the strongest men guarded the broken-spirited Elias. Once filled with bristling gusto, the man was a deflated version of himself. He watched his neighbors throw the rope over a low-hanging tree branch reaching part way over the white-capped water.

"Elias Friske," Emily's father announced, stepping forward and fitting the hemp loop over the old man's head. Friske made no effort to resist his fate, his hands held firm behind his back. "For your sin of murder, a crime against Almighty God, and these people of Laphamville, you shall be hanged. May God have mercy on your soul..." The man's eyes filled with tears. He glanced at the white, wet corpses laid out like little sleeping dolls. *"Damn you!"* The man punctuated his insult by burying his fist into Elias's midsection. Doubling over, the old man coughed, prevented from collapse by the taut rope cinching tight around his neck.

The Laphamites surged forward, pummeling the defenseless man until blood stained their knuckles.

"Enough," called Mother of Caleb. "Let His will be done."

The others obeyed, backing away from the broken man. Three heavy-set brutes each took a length of rope in their bloodied hands. They tugged as one, leaning back on their heels.

The rope squeezed, and Elias choked out, "I shall return! I will be redeemed in the eyes of the faithful! I curse ye wretched souls –!"

Friske was hoisted into the air, feet kicking. Neck stretching, eyes bulging, the purple-faced Elias heard the crack of separating vertebrate. His vision faded into blackness.

Grief-stricken parents gawked at the final twitches as death set in. The brutes anchored the rope to a tree trunk. Friske swayed in the breeze. Branch and hemp fibers creaked, strained by the weight of the condemned. For twenty minutes, they stared.

"Leave him," commanded Emily's father when he saw one of his neighbors pull a knife and grab for the rope. "Let the crows dine."

Mother of Caleb bent down and cradled the head of her only son. She sniffled and wiped her eyes. "Justice is done... now let us tend to our fallen lambs... so they may rest..."

Still children in their arms, the macabre procession snaked its way back toward Laphamville.

#

Storm clouds crept in as darkness descended. Fierce winds, rain, and lightning followed: an expression of God's wrath.

The wind whipped and curled about the stiffening Elias Friske, a puppet on a string, while the River Rogue swelled with flood waters below. Swinging like a heavy pendulum, the stressed rope creaked, beginning to fray.

The rope gave way. Cold flesh splashed into churning rapids.

Friske's colorless face, frozen in a grimace, briefly surfaced before the current carried him away.

CHAPTER 1

HELL OF A BRIDGE

October 25, 2015

Five teenagers gathered on the rusting iron foot bridge spanning the river. A small speaker blared tunes of the newest hip hop single, the teens bobbing their heads.

A wooden sign erected near the bridge warned "DANGER: Keep Away." Beneath the words, a rough "hangman" symbol was carved into the wood.

"Hell of a bridge," commented Stanley Dunbar, unimpressed. Nearly everything was subpar in the eyes of the star quarterback. "This place stinks. Literally! Smells like death out here."

"I thought Melissa cut one," Matthew laughed, pinching his nose. The blurry-eyed stoner fancied himself a clown.

The girl shot him a dirty look.

"It *does* stink like decay," replied Mercedes, who embodied the Goth look with black hair, lips, and nails. "Hunters come out here and leave behind the parts they don't want."

Stanley scoffed. "I told you we should have gone to Findlay Cemetery instead..."

"The Ada Witch legend is bullshit," Mercedes said. "They've debunked that myth."

Stanley, ahead by several beers, walked over the bridge, heel-to-toe, arms outstretched as if walking a tight rope. "Yeah, 'cause this 'Hell's Bridge' seems real legit..." He paused to spit in the water.

"Just give it a chance," said Melissa Osborne, the meticulously groomed A student who liked to flirt with trouble. "Gotta keep an open mind. Who wants to play a game?"

Stanley paused to light a cigarette. "What kind of game? Strip poker?"

"You wish," Melissa replied, rolling her eyes. "I was thinking 'Light as a Feather, Stiff as a Board.'" A collective groan arose from the throats of the others.

"Pfftt," Mercedes dismissed. "That was a fun game... back in middle school."

Melissa pouted. "Just tryin' to liven up this funeral. I'm bored. What do you want to do?"

"I know what *I* want to do," said Matthew, a crooked joint protruding from his lips. He sparked his lighter, touched the flame to the end of his joint, inhaling deeply.

"Big surprise," Melissa jeered. "You're always getting stoned. I want excitement and reality... not an escape from it."

"I'm not escaping reality," Matthew argued between tokes. "I'm *enhancing* it."

"Whatever," Melissa said, fake-coughing, and added under her breath, "Burnout."

"I got a game." Mercedes spoke up with unusual perkiness, wearing a smirk. She patted the tattered canvass bag slung over her shoulder.

Melissa was hopeful. "Yeah?"

Mercedes sat on the bridge, cross legged as she unzipped her bag, digging around. "Say hello to Mr. Ouija." She produced an old Ouija board and its heart-shaped planchette.

It was Melissa's turn to be dismissive. "I've played with those stupid things before..."

"Not like this one," said Mercedes.

Melissa drew closer to her oddball friend, examining

the aged wooden board. "Not like the one my parents bought at MichiMart." Although this version boasted the same twenty six Old English letters, "yes," "no," and "Good Bye" options, its appearance was... uniquely antique.

"This isn't one of those mass-produced pieces of junk. *This* is an heirloom. Belonged to my great grandmother."

"'1864,'" Melissa read the date scratched into the bottom corner.

Raising a suggestive eyebrow, Mercedes asked, "Wanna play?"

Melissa hesitated. "I dunno..."

Stanley belched, reminding the others of his presence. He chucked an empty can into the water. It splashed and bobbed like a cork as it drifted away until swallowed by darkness.

"What're you scared of?"

"I don't know..." Melissa was apprehensive. "It's just extra creepy."

"Be careful," spoke Jennifer, the quiet girl from a strict Catholic Polish family. "You're messing with a form of Divination. Dabbling in dark stuff can come back at you."

"Oooohh," Matthew laughed, wiggling his hands. "Oogey boogey's gonna getchya!"

"I'm serious," said Jennifer. "You think it's just a

game, but those things are like doorways... portals to another world." She toyed with the crucifix hanging from her neck.

"Who should we conjure?" Mercedes asked, biting her lip. "Ideas?"

"I got one," Stanley said nonchalantly. He retrieved a beer from the half-empty case. "Maybe you've heard of him." He paused for dramatic effect. *"Elias Friske."*

"Oh gawd," Matthew groaned.

"Perfect," Mercedes purred.

"Who's Elias Friske?" asked Melissa, intrigued.

Jennifer gave a look of disgust. "You mean the child killer? You guys are sick. You shouldn't joke around about that."

Melissa asked, "This Friske guy killed children?"

"About a dozen," Mercedes informed. "A long time ago... before Rockford was Rockford, this area was 'Laphamville.' Not long after the land was settled, some children in the village went missing. When the parents went out to look for them, they left the rest of their little ones with a trusted town elder... a man supposedly of God, a man they could trust unconditionally... "

"Friske?" Melissa asked, knowing the answer. Mercedes nodded.

"The parents of Laphamville looked all day, and found

no trace of the kids. When they returned to the village, Friske and the other children were gone.

They went back into the woods, and found Elias, not far from this exact spot... blood-covered, babbling about demons." Mercedes paused, allowing her words to sink in. "The parents demanded to know what had become of their children. Elias led them here..." The girl pointed to a twisted old tree on the far side of the bridge. "That's when they saw... children floating in the river... dead... tied together with rope..."

"Then what happened?"

"They lynched him. Right there, from that very tree."

Melissa shivered. "Gives me the chills!"

"Bullshit," Stanley chuckled. "How do know you that?"

Mercedes ignored him. "It was right there. They strung him up, watched him die, and left the body to rot."

The group grew quiet, trying to recreate the event in their minds.

"Well, what are we waiting for?" Matthew broke the silence. "Let's ring him up, see what he's been up to the last hundred years."

The smile stretched across Mercedes' pale face grew mischievous. "Want to?"

"NO!" Jennifer objected. "*Don't.* I know you guys want

Halloween fun, but you're on thin ice. Don't mess with stuff you don't understand."

"You're free to leave if you're too scared, sweetie," sneered Mercedes. She resented the pseudo-authority from Jennifer. She added under her breath, "Party pooper."

The comment sent Jennifer into a rage. "Screw it! I'm going home. You think I'm just a stick-in-the-mud, but I'm just trying to look out for you guys. You don't know what you're dealing with!" The young woman gathered her purse before standing up. "Don't say I didn't warn you."

"Bye, bye! Sleep tight," called Mercedes in a mocking voice. Jennifer thought about flipping her the bird, but being a good Christian, she suppressed the impulse. Instead, she screwed her face up into the meanest, dirtiest look she could muster, casting daggers from her eyes at Mercedes. She stomped off through the mud into the darkness.

"Want me to walk you home?" Stanley asked, half-serious.

"I'm fine, thanks," Jennifer answered, already lost in the dark.

"Good riddance," remarked Mercedes. She held up the Ouija board. "Who wants to do this?"

"Me!!" Matthew raised his hand.

"I'm in," said Stanley, helping himself to a seat next to

Melissa. They made eye contact. "You?"

"Sure," she shrugged. "Nothing will happen as long as we're all here together, right?"

Stanley took the opportunity to slip his arm around Melissa. "You bet." She immediately brushed his arm away.

"Okay, guys," Mercedes announced, trying to marshal their attention. "Gather 'round. Let's see if this Elias Friske is still out here, and... no cheating."

"Promise," Stanley pledged.

"Here we go," Mercedes exhaled slowly. All four leaned in, fingertips on the planchette. "Hear me, Elias Friske! I summon thee! Give us a sign..."

The river gurgled. The trees swayed gently in a phantom breeze, limbs creaking.

A lone bird screeched in the distance, calling to the night.

"This is creeping me out," Melissa said. "The hairs on the back of my neck just stood up!"

"You're psyching yourself out," chided Stanley.

"Ask him something, Mercedes," Matthew urged.

"ELIAS FRISKE!" Mercedes shouted, making the others jump. "Are you there?"

They all waited, watching for movement of the planchette. It began to slide to the upper left corner of the board.

"Quit movin' it, Stan," Melissa said.

"I'm not," Stanley said. "I swear."

It stopped.

Its answer: YES.

"Did the children of Laphamville die by your hand?" asked Mercedes.

The planchette moved several inches to the right, and then returned to the YES option.

"This is stupid!" Matthew exclaimed, pulling his hand back from the board. "Stan keeps moving it!"

"Fuck you, pothead!" Stanley stood, fists balled. "I *wasn't* moving it."

"Well, *someone* was."

Silence.

"Maybe it was Elias Friske...?" Stanley was mocking him now.

Mercedes added gravely, "Maybe it was."

"Go to Hell, Stan."

Stanley's face suddenly shifted from a taunting pout to genuine fear. "Matthew, don't move. There's something behind you..."

Matthew's muscles tensed. Slowly, he cast a glance over his shoulder. As he did, Stanley leaned forward, socking him in the shoulder.

"Ouch!"

"Made you look, pussy," Stanley chuckled as Matthew rubbed the point of impact.

"Knock it off guys," admonished Melissa. "Come on, let's try again."

"Let's not," Stanley said.

"Please?" Melissa begged. Her voice melted Stanley's tough exterior. He gave up and resumed his sitting position next to the blonde.

"Ask him something else." Stanley's suggested.

This time Matthew asked, "Elias Friske... do you regret what you did?"

Transfixed, the four saw the planchette quiver in place before zipping across to the opposite side of the board.

It stopped.

NO.

"Holy shit," Mercedes said. The swiftness of the movement took them all by surprise. "Can't be any clearer than that. Melissa, want to ask something?"

"Why... did you do it, Elias?" Melissa asked, stuttering. "Why kill little children?" The others watched with great interest as the planchette began its journey.

First letter: L.

Second letter: U.

Third letter: S.

Fourth, letter: T.

"'Lust?' What's that supposed to mean...? He was a pervert, too?"

"I don't think that's what he meant," Mercedes opined. She again led the makeshift séance. "Elias Friske: Did you abuse those children before you took their lives?"

The planchette travelled back to the NO position. Without further asking, the planchette traversed the alphabet. It paused briefly over the letters, B, L, U, T.

"Blut? That's not even a word," giggled Matthew. "What an idiot ghost."

"No, not 'blut,'" Mercedes repeated Matthew's pronunciation in a hillbilly accent. "'Blut.'" She pronounced it "bloot." "It's German for 'blood.'"

"Oh really, Frau Nazi? How do you know that?"

"Great grandma's second husband was from Bonn. She used to make him blutwurst on his birthday, it was his favorite. Only after I ate some did she tell me it was 'blood wurst,' or congealed blood sausage."

"Gag me with a stick," Melissa said with a sour face. "Gross."

"It wasn't bad," Mercedes added. "So... lust and blood. Lust blood. Blood lust." She nodded vigorously, assured of her revelation. "That's got to be it. Blood lust - he was blood thirsty."

"He *drank* their blood... like a vampire?"

"Nein," Mercedes flaunted her limited bilingualism. "I think he meant metaphorically."

"Right," Stanley agreed. He whispered in Melissa's ear, "Like if I say I could eat you up, I don't mean I'd cut a chunk off your body, put it on the grill, and smother it with BBQ sauce."

The annoyed blonde shoved him away again. "Sick. Keep your innuendos, and your hands, to yourself."

"Let's keep going," Mercedes suggested. "Things are starting to get interesting."

"Gotta drain the lizard." Stanley stood up, looking at Matthew. "Wanna give me a hand? Doctor says I shouldn't do any heavy lifting." He walked away, laughing.

"I *hate* him," Matthew said. The sound of a zipper and then trickling water came from the other side of the foot bridge.

Melissa seconded the declaration. "He's a douche bag."

"Holy shit!" Stanley screamed.

"What? Did it shrink even more?" giggled Melissa.

"Is the rash back again?" Matthew joined the teasing.

Stanley ran back, the rickety bridge clanking under his shoes. "I just saw a pair of eyes."

Matthew giggled. He began to sing, "Sometimes I feel like, somebody's watching meeeee...."

"Shut up, Matt. I swear on my soul, I saw two red eyes moving around between the trees."

"Sure you did," Matthew teased.

SPLASH! A cold, wet hand reached up from the water, grabbing Melissa's ankle. She struggled against the firm grip, twisting, trying to get away. "Someone's got me!"

Both young men leapt to the aid of Melissa, grabbing her under the arms, trying to wrench her free.

Mercedes produced a shiny stiletto from her handbag – her self-defense weapon of choice. She bent and stabbed the hand that held her friend.

"AAHH!" Whoever was hidden below let out a very earthly scream.

Matthew and Stanley pulled Melissa away from danger.

A tiny projectile, the size of a toothpick, sailed through the air, and stuck into Stanley's neck.

"What the fu-" His jaw locked. Every muscle seized. He fell, stiff, face-first into the water.

Mercedes screamed. She dropped the stiletto, and

21

sprinted toward the woods. The bridge creaked and bounced under her booted feet, and then she was on solid ground.

Blind in the dark, she didn't see the baseball bat that hit her face. Bone and cartilage snapped. She fell backward.

Her head smacked the bridge. She lay delirious and defenseless as hands descended on her. Thumbs dug into her mascara-lined eyes, pressing, shoving, corkscrewing, until cuticle met eye socket.

In the center of the bridge, Matthew huddled, holding Melissa in white-knuckled terror.

"I'll protect you," Matthew said, and was suddenly choked as a leather strap wrapped around his neck. It yanked him away from the girl, unbalancing him. He fell backward into the water, gurgling. He did not resurface.

Alone, crying, Melissa wet her pants. Her trembling hand searched for her cell phone. She found it, frantically swiping her index finger across the screen.

Something heavy struck her skull, splitting it open.

Melissa fell forward, phone flying from her hand. It bounced once off the iron grating, and flopped, screen facing up, onto the muddy riverbank.

As dark, shapeless forms converged on the girl, the screen on her phone blinked.

A new text message: "Don't be out too late. Love, Mom."

CHAPTER 2
BIGFOOT HUNTER

The microwave dinged, alerting Birgil Doxey that dinner was ready. He cleared space on the overcrowded dining room table, which doubled as his workspace. Birgil grabbed the hot tray before ripping off the cellophane covering.

Without looking, he snatched a plastic fork amongst the mess that was his countertop. His eyes never left the black and white TV screen perched on the corner of the table.

"Local authorities are still trying to determine the whereabouts of four missing teenagers near the Rockford area," reported a newscaster standing at the foot of Hell's Bridge. "This bridge behind me, known to local residents as 'Hell's Bridge,' was the last place missing teens Melissa Osborne, Merecedes Vesser, Stanley Dunbar, and Matthew

Boley were seen late last night.

According to sixteen-year-old Jennifer Salinski, who claims to have left the area around 11:30 last night, her friends were attempting to conjure the spirit of Elias Friske. Friske, a suspected child killer, was lynched near this bridge by vengeful parents back in the 1800s. Salinski is still being held for questioning by local law enforcement."

"Hell's Bridge," Birgil repeated as he dug into a watery helping of mashed potatoes. As a paranormal investigator and self-described crypto-zoologist, his interest piqued at the mention of the local haunt site.

"There has been rampant speculation as to the fate of the missing four," the reporter added. "Police have yet to rule out foul play, and their department spokesperson has not issued a statement as detectives continue to probe the case. However, an anonymous source has confirmed human blood was found at the scene."

Birgil swallowed the last bite of brown goo-smothered Salisbury steak, chased it with flat root beer, and belched. "Sounds like a case for Birgil Doxey."

Shoving his camouflage boonie hat on his head, Birgil opened a drawer next to the sink, pulling out a holstered .40 caliber Smith & Wesson. He stuffed the weapon under his belt at his hip, adjusting his stained shirt over the bulge. He switched off the light, and snatched up his work bag and keys before walking out the door.

#

Crouching, Birgil plucked a cigarette butt from the mud with a pair of tweezers. He dropped it into a plastic baggie that also contained bottle caps, a candy wrapper, and a hair tie: clues salvaged from the moist ground near Hell's Bridge.

Shirt over his nose, Doxey pocketed the bag, fiddling with his EMF meter. The place stunk to high heaven, like a struck match - a sulfur smell. An annoying tone from his device didn't signal changes in the electromagnetic field, but rather a dying battery.

"Damn thing," cursed the investigator. He was certain he'd charged the meter the night before. *Maybe my memory is slipping,* he thought.

Sounds of footsteps on the bridge. Birgil froze, scanned his surroundings. Nothing.

He glanced the DANGER sign, did a double take, focusing on the crude symbol etched into the wood.

"Hangman?" thought Doxey aloud. Straight, sketchy lines formed a stick figure hanging by its neck.

He recognized the symbol, and not as an innocent kid's game. He tapped a finger against his chin. *Where had he seen it before?*

"The *Hangman*," Doxey said. He recalled the unknown serial killer police tracked in the area, but that was nearly forty years ago. Seemingly random victims were found hanging by their necks, the peculiar symbol carved into chests and stomachs. Despite multiple leads, the case remained cold at the Algoma Township Police Department.

The squawk of a siren startled Birgil, causing him to jump, whacking his head against a low-hanging tree branch.

"You've got no business here, Bigfoot hunter," called a policeman in plainclothes, exiting the squad car.

Birgil straightened, rubbing his head. "'Cuse me? My name is Birgil Doxey."

The policeman, a brown fedora on his head and gleaming badge on his belt, struggled down the embankment toward the bridge. He tried to point his finger as he spoke, but had to use the hand instead to steady his bulky frame.

"I know who you are," the cop said, winded. "You're that fellow who goes out looking for Bigfoot, 'n aliens, 'n ghosts, n' shit."

"I prefer 'paranormal investigator.'"

"You're a weirdo who creeps people out," the cop retorted. "And you're disturbin' a crime scene. See the yellow tape?!"

27

Birgil glanced around the bridge. Yellow police tape flipped and fluttered in the breeze, including the cut section where he had entered. He cleared his throat, "Must've missed it," and quickly added, "What crime occurred?"

The detective sighed. "We don't know... yet. Concerned citizens saw you come down here and phoned it in. They don't want you pokin' around, and neither do I!"

"My apologies, officer...?"

"*Detective* Brazo. Algoma PD."

"They normally send detectives out for a call like that?"

"I'm in charge of the investigation. Wanted to check you out myself."

"I only know what the news reported. I wanted to see if there was anything you might have overlooked."

"Overlooked?" Brazo laughed. "We're professionals; not amateur shadow chasers."

Doxey sighed. "Paranormal investigator."

"To me, you're a pain in the ass. We don't need you sticking your nose where it don't belong. You need to leave."

Birgil opened his mouth, then noticed the detective move a hand down to a holstered pistol and leather pouch containing handcuffs.

"Fine," Doxey threw up his hands. "Just trying to help." He turned and scampered up the embankment toward the main road, and his waiting Toyota. He didn't want to give the cop a chance to second-guess his decision.

Detective Brazo looked on disapprovingly.

CHAPTER 3
HOME, SWEET HOME

Unlocking the door to his apartment, Birgil hurried inside. He re-locked the door, turned on the kitchen light. He grabbed for the chair in front of the table, but it was not in its usual spot. A creature of habit, he *always* pushed in his chair when he stood up, mental training retained from grade school.

Someone had moved it.

A chill crept up Birgil's spine as he checked the rest of the apartment. He noticed nothing out of place. When he opened the refrigerator for a can of bargain brand cola, he saw something else. The gallon of milk was... half empty.

"I just bought that this morning," Doxey said disbelievingly. "You're losing it, Birgil."

Hairs on his arms stood up, chilled from a source other

than the refrigerator. From the window. A white curtain flapped in the wind.

Birgil never left his windows open. *Someone* had been in his apartment, but who? Nothing was missing. His late father's gold watch lay untouched near the bathroom sink. If the work of thieves, they were terrible at what they did.

"Maybe I scared them off?" His gaze went to the food and water dishes at his feet. "Fluffy? Here kitty, kitty, kitty..." Room by room, he checked his cat's favorite hiding spots. No sign of the feline. Almost as jarring as the thought of a stranger in his home, he realized his beloved pet may have escaped through the open window...

"Gotta call it in, I suppose," he said, picking up his cordless phone.

The line was dead. Birgil held the phone away from his face, checking the battery. Fully charged. Still no dial tone.

Thoroughly spooked, he took his keys, double-checked the door locks, and left the building.

CHAPTER 4
COP SHOP

Sitting in Detective Kane Brazo's air conditioned office, Birgil regretted not grabbing his windbreaker as he left the apartment. He had a perpetual chill since he discovered his home had been violated.

With his fedora on the desk next to a steaming coffee mug, the detective scribbled notes on his legal pad. He paused occasionally for a quick sip.

"Dead phone, chair moved, open window, missing cat," Brazo read off. "Got it. Strange, though... no other reports of B and E's in your building, or anywhere else in the neighborhood, for that matter. You sure it's not a personal thing? An old girl friend who forgot to give your key back?"

"Never given my key to anyone."

"Probably just some kids who tested your window, got

in, and raided your fridge. Who else is going to drink a half gallon of milk?

There's not a whole lot we can do in this situation, I'm afraid. We've got your report on file here. I can see about stepping up patrols near your area. Otherwise, this appears to be an isolated incident. Sorry about your missing cat. Hope you find him."

"Her," Birigil corrected. "And thanks."

"Anything else?" Doxey shook his head. The detective sat his fedora on his head, and led the paranormal investigator toward the exit. "I'll keep you posted if we hear anything."

"Thanks, I appreciate it," Doxey shook the man's hand. As he turned to leave, he noticed his Toyota was not how he left it. "What the Hell--" He rushed out the door, Brazo hot on his heels.

Birgil stood before his vehicle, mouth agape, surveying the damage. "Oh... my..."

All four tires were flat. A dark red liquid, which he rightfully believed to be blood, covered his windshield.

"You sure as Hell pissed off *somebody*," Brazo commented. "Positive you don't have a lover scorned?"

"Doubt it." Birgil noticed writing scratched into the paint job. Odd, foreign words. "What's this...?"

"'*Graviora Manent,*'" the detective read. "Latin. Means 'greater dangers await.'"

Doxey looked at Brazo, surprised. "Didn't know the Algoma PD trained their people in the use of Latin."

"Learned it at St. Agatha's School for Boys. Looks like someone has it out for you, Mr. Doxey."

Annoyed, Birgil answered, "It appears so, doesn't it?" He pointed to a surveillance camera atop a light pole in the parking lot. "Can we review the security tape?"

"Oh, that?" laughed the detective. "It's a dummy camera. A 'crime deterrent.' Non-functioning empty box."

"Just my luck." Palm smacked forehead.

"Township board turned down our request for an updated system," Brazo informed. "Not 'financially feasible.'"

"Perfect."

"They didn't just let the air of your tires," observed Brazo, bending down. "They slashed 'em. We'll have to get your truck towed to a service station... can't have a blood-covered vehicle sitting in our parking lot. Doesn't look right." Birgil rubbed his temples, trying to massage away the impending headache. "I can give you a lift home."

"Think it's safe for me to go home?"

"Just exercise vigilance. Keep your doors and windows

locked. Be aware of anything or anyone unusual."

"I'm not scared," Birgil asserted.

"Never said you were."

"I've got a concealed carry permit, but my lack of a working phone concerns me. What if I need to call you in a hurry?"

"Wait here," Brazo held up a finger, retreating into the police station. Minutes later, he walked out holding a black electronic device. "Here. Emergency cell phone. Only calls to 911 will go through."

"Thanks," muttered Doxey as he took the flip phone. "You just *give* these things out?"

"Part of a state program to ensure low-income and elderly folks have a way to call for help."

"Hopefully I won't need it. Let me grab some stuff outta the truck before they take it away." He ducked inside and gathered his personal belongings. "How am I going to clean this up?"

"We've got paper towels in the men's room." The detective grinned, his way of saying "your problem, not mine."

In his best imitation of an English accent, Birgil lowered his head and said, "Bloody Hell."

CHAPTER 5

NIGHT DANCE

Despite phone and firearm, Birgil still didn't feel safe at home. More like a prisoner. He needed to get out of there. With his truck in the shop, he knew he'd be hoofing it. The exercise and fresh air won't kill me, he thought.

Admiring the vibrant orange, yellow, purple, and red leaves, Birgil strolled eastward down 12 Mile Road. Every porch he passed boasted combinations of carved pumpkins, dried corn stalks, and broomstick-riding witches. As suburbia turned to farmland, the homes were spread farther apart. He inhaled the sweet scent of apples.

For reasons he couldn't explain, Birgil trekked north, down Friske Drive. The winding dirt road led him to a gravel turnaround. He felt drawn by some force unseen, and approximately 200 yards down the overgrown trail, he found himself back at Hell's Bridge. There had to be more to this story. He was determined to get to the bottom of it.

Who was after him? The "Hangman?" The ghost of Elias Friske?

Birgil snapped a dozen pictures, hoping to capture "orbs," or signs of ectoplasm. He saw nothing as he scrolled through photos. The battery icon on the camera warned: "BATT 12%, Connect Charger." As with his EMF reader, the fully-charged device drained much too fast.

Feeling hopeless, he sat on the iron bridge, staring at the water. He let his mind wander.

Strange noises in the distance. Whooping, hollering, laughing. A party in progress? No, not drunken merriment. The sounds were odder, darker – drumming, chanting.

Birgil curiously journeyed down a long-neglected railroad stretching into the horizon.

He followed the tracks, toward the chanting. As he trudged farther from civilization, he saw light cast from a bonfire, illuminating a clearing in the woods. The flames weren't orange-red, but a strange electric blue.

Doxey crouched behind a tree, hidden by its shadow as he observed the gathering. His skin tingled.

People dressed in black robes, others naked, danced in a circle- blazing blue bonfire their hub. Behind the fire stood a makeshift altar –candles, incense, coils of black beads, a stone gargoyle figurine, and an aged wooden Ouija board, atop which sat a stark white skull. Dangling from the crates were dozens of small animals, stiff, decomposing. Lengths of twine secured the mummified creatures, suspending them by their necks. Bats flew overhead, flapping wings silhouetted against moonlight.

They chanted in an unfamiliar language. Each person continued to hop, dance, and spin around the altar. All except one – a thin man, early 20's, stripped to the waist. His chest scarred by a large hangman symbol, legs encased in leather pants, and head topped with spiky red hair. Head bowed, as if praying, he remained oblivious to the commotion. The man's nostrils flared, sniffing the air.

"HALT," barked spiky-haired leader. Like trained soldiers, the others froze. The man inhaled deeply, "... an *outsider...* is in our midst!" Head still bent, the man raised an index finger, pointing directly at Birgil's hiding spot.

"AWAY!" In a whirlwind of swishing robes and grabbing hands, the altar was disassembled in seconds. The lead cultist clutched the skull with both hands, cradled in his midsection.

POP! A smoke grenade filled the area with choking clouds. The thick gray plume washed over the crouching investigator. Eyes watering, he coughed, spit. Looking up, he saw the cult had vanished.

Doxey noticed the recently-raging blue fire now extinguished. Smoldering embers were all that remained.

Willing himself forward, he noticed dozens of shriveled rabbit heads, a hallowed deer carcass, and a mangled mass of red-stained white fur. A small purple collar embedded in the mud. He picked it up, stretching it out.

Doxey whispered the name on the collar. "Fluffy..." He took out his emergency phone, dialing 911.

"911, what's your emergency?"

"Transfer me to the Algoma Police Department."

"What's the nature of your emergency?"

"Transfer me, NOW!"

"One moment," said the annoyed 911 operator.

"Algoma Township dispatch," answered a voice.

"I need to speak with Detective Kane Brazo – it's urgent."

"Who is this?"

"Tell him it's the Bigfoot Hunter." Silence; the policeman wasn't sure if the call was a Halloween prank. "Nevermind. Tell him it's Birgil Doxey. He knows who I am."

"One second."

A tired voice came over the line. "Hello, Mr. Doxey."

"Detective," Birgil said, fighting tears. "... I know what happened to Fluffy."

CHAPTER 6

PLAYING WITH FIRE

On the walk home, Birgil was haunted by the thought of his kitty meeting her demise from the cultists. A grumbling stomach forced him to make a brief food stop before returning to his apartment. Watching the weather forecast, he wolfed down his Mitten Burger in record time. Mouth crammed full of fries, he was surprised to hear the phone ring.

Must have repaired the line while I was out, he thought. It was the car repair center, calling to say his Toyota's tires were replaced. It was ready for pick up. He'd get it in the morning, he decided.

The extra-greasy, sodium-heavy meal churned in his guts. An oncoming food coma sent him to bed, yet he couldn't find rest. He tossed and turned, disturbed by the bizarre set of occurrences. The bloody truck, the naked forest dancers, the blue flame... the hangman symbol.

In only his underwear, Birgil stumbled out to his desk. He started searching the internet, looking for any information he could find about the "Hangman" cold cases. He found nothing.

Three extra- strength pain killers later, Birgil gave sleep another try.

#

The next day, Doxey walked to the service station, thankful to have his truck back. He drove straight to the Algoma Township Library, hoping they would have the answers he sought.

Again, a brick wall. The library had purged their hard copies of old newspapers; everything was *digitized* now. No stories about the "Hangman."

All hope lost, Birgil lingered by the front doors, looking over the bulletin board. Above, a line of faded framed portraits. Wrinkly bald men in suits. A brass plate over the photos read, "Algoma Township Historical Society." The men were past presidents.

Doxey, searching with his index finger, found the president of the society from 1978 to 1992 – a smiling gentleman: Walter N. Mendall. He figured Mendall, if alive, would have heard about the "Hangman" cases. But, how to find him? The Yellow Pages?

"Excuse me, miss?"

The frumpy, bespectacled woman behind the counter looked up from her book. "Can I help you?"

"I'm looking for Mr. Mendall, used to head the historical society..."

She had the look of staring into fog. "No, I'm sorry..."

"Oh, you mean Walter?" asked a second woman, a beautiful teenage nerd. She'd been bent down, organizing a shelf. "That's Lilly's granddad." She paused, and explained. "Lilly's my friend. I'm think her grandpa's still kickin', but doesn't live on his own..."

"Any way you could find out? I need to speak with him."

"Sure," the girl chirped. She dug a phone from her back pocket, began poking at it.

"You *are* on the clock, Alanna," the stern librarian reminded. Alanna looked to Birgil, eyes begging understanding.

"Can I go on break...?"

The frump frowned harder, but relented. "Fine. Thirty minutes," she reminded, tapping her watch.

Birgil struggled to keep pace with the spunky Alanna,

following her to the parking lot. He watched her dig a pack of cigarettes from her purse. Once lit, she drew heavily, savoring, then blew a thick cloud. "She can be *such* a bitch sometimes..."

"Seemed pleasant to me," Doxey said, smirking.

"I'll call Lilly. What did you say your name was...?"

"Birgil Doxey, but her grandpa doesn't know me. It's about some local history."

"Huh," answered Alanna, uninterested. She was relieved when her friend answered. "Hey Lilly, it's me. Listen, I'm on break at work right now, and there's this guy here who wants to talk to your grandpa."

Doxey heard the other girl ask, "what for?"

"Wants to talk to him about... history, or something. Says his name is..." She looked to him to fill in the blank.

"Birgil Doxey," he enunciated.

"Virgil Boxey," Alanna repeated. "Seems fine. Just wants to talk; I'm sure grandpa would enjoy a visit."

#

Birgil's beefy frame filled the doorway. Staring at the pale, emaciated shell of a man curled in the recliner, he couldn't believe it was the same individual in the framed photo at the library. Time had been cruel to Walter Mendell.

Eyes closed, mouth open, it wasn't clear if the man was alive. Mendell wasn't dead – yet. Shallow breathing indicated life. A string of drool vibrated by the rattle of an occasional snort.

"Go on, hon." The voice came from the busty blonde nurse standing at his side. "He's just resting." Her drawl indicated a southern upbringing. Doxey inhaled the sweet scent of her perfume, a welcomed contrast to the sickly stench of puss, phlegm, and death.

"You sure?"

The nurse approached the sleeping old timer, bent down, and gently shook the man's shoulder. "Walter, wake up, darlin'. You have a visitor." Doxey observed, enjoying the view of the nurse from behind.

Walter's head jerked, eyes snapped open. "What?!" Sitting up, he wiped his mouth.

"You have a visitor, Walter. This is..."

"Birgil Doxey." The investigator stepped forward to offer his hand.

Walter's glazed eyes stared. "I'll let you two talk." The nurse turned and walked from the room, both men watching her gluteus maximus.

"What do you want from me?" Walter asked, tugging a quilt over his lap.

"Answers." Birgil helped himself to a seat.

"Brain's all dried up," Walter pointed to his liver-spotted forehead. "Ain't nothin' left up here 'cept moths and crickets."

"I doubt that," Doxey said, grinning. "You were the president of the Algoma Township Historical Society..."

"I was?" Walter twisted his mouth, scratching a scab on his bald dome. He laughed. "Just pullin' your chain. I remember."

"What do you remember about the 'Hangman?'"

"The what?" Walter cupped his ear.

"*Hangman.* Unsolved murders in the area back in the 80s...? Hanging bodies...? Ring a bell?"

Walter rubbed his chin, thinking. His index finger shot into the air. "You mean *'the Faithful!'* That's who it was – the Faithful!"

He's lost it, Doxey thought. "I think you're confused..."

"Don't talk down to me, tubby. I still got my marbles! There was *no* 'Hangman.' That was some bullshit story the cops cooked up to feed reporters."

"Why would they lie?"

"They didn't want to look incompetent. They made up that crap about the 'Hangman' so it looked like they had a clue. It was the Faithful."

"Who're the Faithful?"

"A cult I guess you'd call them. Underground weirdoes who worshipped the spirit of some baby killer."

"'Underground?' Like off the grid?"

"No, like subterranean. Literally *under* the ground. They lived in little hideouts dug out of the earth, connected by a series of tunnels. Called themselves the 'Faithful.' Led by some Kraut guru who believed certain folks needed to be sacrificed in order to appease their child-killer messiah."

"Who was the child-killer messiah?"

"Some psycho who lived around here in the 1800s. He supposedly killed a bunch of local kids. The parents got together and stretched his neck... I forget the name."

"You're talking about the legend of Hell's Bridge, right? Elias Friske?"

"Yes! That was the bastard's name. But the legend's fake– not a shred of truth to it. *However,* some immigrant named Hans Kaltenbrunner believed the story. He was the son of a Nazi war criminal who snuck over after the war. Friske was a Kraut too, so he felt a natural kinship to him."

"You can take the boy out of the Reich, but you can't take the Reich out of the boy?'"

Walter nodded. A look of fear and paranoia washed over the older man's features. Squinting his eyes, he scanned the room for shadows. His voice a whisper, "Kaltenbrunner felt Friske was some sort of dark prophet, sent to earth to carry out the will of the Prince of Demons. He bought the legend hook, line, and sinker.

He found others, winos, junkies, or runaways, who believed the story too. He started his own quasi-religion, with Friske as their holy -*or unholy*- man. Kaltenbrunner called his little flock the 'Faithful.' They carved out their own little dirt kingdom, right beneath the feet of the honest folks of Rockford."

"No shit..." Birgil shook his head.

"Crazy, right? Those folks killed back then, they weren't just random strangers like the police made it out. They had something in common: each had a relative involved in the Faithful. They tried to get their loved ones out. To Kaltenbrunner, these people were a threat, so he had them killed in the same fashion as their prophet."

"How do *you* know about this group?"

"I was working for the paper at the time," Mendell explained. "Investigative journalist. My editor threatened to can my ass if I even submitted that 'garbage theory' for print. The dumb bastard went on and on about how he personally knew the chief of police, and how he was a competent professional, and above all, an honest Christian man."

"Didn't believe him?"

"Not for a minute. They shouldn't have ignored it – the pieces were right there in front of them. I have a theory, though..."

"Knock-knock," called the busty nurse from the doorway, paper cup in hand. "Sorry to interrupt, but Walter, it's time for your medicine."

The old man turned away. "Don't bother," Walter said. "They don't do a damn thing for me anyway."

"You still gotta take 'em. They keep you outta trouble." The nurse held the cup out. "Please? For me...?" Her voice was just too damn sweet. Even for an old fart like Walter, who hadn't felt the masculine stir down below in decades, she still had an attractive quality to her.

A swallow of warm water later, the pills were gone. Mendell crumpled the paper cup before tossing it into the waste basket. He folded his arms, scowling. "Happy?"

She smiled warmly, bent down, and planted a kiss on Mendell's wrinkled forehead. "Thank you, hon."

"Where was I?" asked Mendell once the nurse made her exit.

"You had a theory..."

"Oh, yes. My theory: Kaltenbrunner's gang of oddballs was not what it seemed. They were the tip of the spear, or the iceberg – the visible head above the surface. I think the whole power establishment around Rockford was –*and is*-infested with the Faithful. The whole town's in on it. Mayors, police chiefs, *newspaper editors.* All had an interest in protecting this group."

"Walter, I think the Faithful are still active."

"Of course they are! Their leader died back in '95 – I can still picture his ugly mug in the obits. They quieted down after that, but they're... still out there."

"I think *I* may be their target this time," Doxey admitted. He went on to explain the recent events at Hell's Bridge. Walter sat back, nodding. None of it shocked him.

Story finished, Doxey stared, awaiting feedback. "What should I do?"

"Be *very* careful," Mendell finally spoke. He struggled with his words, which seemed caught in his throat. "You're playing with fire, Mr. Doxey. These people will stop at nothing. They'll go to any lengths to protect their members – you've seen that." The old man stopped, interrupted by a tickling cough. He hacked and coughed, but couldn't clear the obstruction.

"Water?" Birgil took a Styrofoam cup, filling it at the sink. "Here."

"Thank you," the man acknowledged, breathing

labored. "Seriously, watch your ass." Cough, cough. "They've got you in their sights." More coughing. Another drink of water. "Got a gun?"

Birgil nodded. "Got my concealed carry license a few years back." He was concerned Mendell was on the brink of a respiratory episode. His gut urged him to get going.

More coughing. "Good," choked Mendell. He smacked his chest with his fist. His voice now a wheeze, "Don't... be afraid... to... use it." His face turned a purplish hue. The coughing now out of control, Birgil panicked. He wanted to leave, but knew he couldn't.

Poking his head out in the hallway, he hollered, "Nurse! We need some help in here!"

A different nurse, an overweight Hispanic gal, nodded glumly, striding toward the room. No quick hurry.

"She's coming," Doxey turned to report to Mendell. The man sank into the recliner, puckered face now blue. His body shook with spasms, muscles convulsing. Spittle flew from his lips, struggling to breathe. Birgil felt helpless.

"Wait out here, *por favor*," instructed the nurse, ushering him into the hallway. She turned back, and along with busty nurse, attended to Mendell. The man's convulsions ceased, body still. No more attempted breaths. The nurses simply stared, and then set about tidying the room.

Enraged by their lack of compassion, Doxey stormed back into the room. "Aren't you going to do anything?!"

"Too late," the Hispanic nurse shook her head. "Nothing to do."

"She's right," admitted the busty nurse. "He's a goner. We've seen it a thousand times. We'll see it a hundred more times before the week's out. Part of the cycle of life, hon." Realizing her words came off as cold and unfeeling, she approached Birgil, touching his arm. The other nurse slipped into the hallway. "I'm sorry for your loss."

"What?! He was just talking..."

The Hispanic nurse returned, wheeling a stretcher. The ladies hefted Mendell's body onto the stretcher, using his pajamas as handles. They plopped him down like slab of beef.

The busty nurse grunted, slightly dismayed by the death, as she pulled the walkie-talkie from her hip. "Bed in room 215 is now available," she spoke. "Give us thirty to clear out personal belongings."

Birgil stood there, numb, shocked. With dead eyes, he watched the women go about their business.

What he couldn't see, just below busty nurse's left buttock - the tattoo.

A stick figure hanging by its neck.

CHAPTER 7

NIGHT TERROR

"Not much of a turnout," Doxey said to the only other witness at the funeral – the president of the Golden Acres Nursing Home, who only showed up because he felt a moral obligation to do so.

"Family doesn't give a damn." The man was right. After Doxey watched Walter Mendell expire right in front of him, he felt the least he could do was phone the man's granddaughter. He was appalled when Lilly Mendell explained she couldn't make it because she had a salon appointment. Heartless, Doxey thought.

"Though I walk through the valley of the shadow of death, I shall fear no evil..." A volunteer from the local church read from the Bible.

In no mood to converse with the stranger, Doxey stared

at Mendell's coffin as it lowered six feet below, remembering the man's dying warning. "They'll stop at nothing."

\#

Doxey tossed and turned. He fluffed his pillow, forcing eyes shut, yet sleep remained elusive. He'd seen too much in the past days to turn it off.

Glancing at the alarm clock on his bedside table, next to his holstered pistol, Birgil breathed a frustrated sigh. 2:42 AM.

Maybe he should have gotten hammered when he got home. That's what "normal" people did after a shitty day, right? They drank away their problems until they passed out...

The thought gave him an idea.

After relieving his constricted bladder, Birgil sauntered over to the refrigerator. He searched the freezer for a frosted bottle of Vodka. Not the good stuff, the cheapest brand found on the bottom shelf at the liquor store.

He found the bottle of Vladimir's Finest, unscrewed the cap, and brought it to his lips. The potent smell stung his nose, evoking memories of over-consumption in years past. He fought his gag reflex.

Birgil was not a drinker. But this was not for pleasure; it was a necessary indulgence so he could rest. Sleeping medicine. Just as when he was a child, he wasn't eager to swallow the foul-tasting stuff, yet he knew he must.

Half a bottle later, Doxey cut himself off. He cringed, fought the waves of nausea, and replaced the cap. Now he was good and drunk. Standing up, the room spun, and he sank back into the chair.

"I tink yoof ad tooooo mush," Birgil slurred. He turned to a wrinkled poster pinned to the wall. Curled at the corners, it depicted a UFO hovering in place. It bore the phrase: THE TRUTH IS OUT THERE. "Ish it?" he asked.

Steadying himself on table, he stood, and replaced the vodka.

Now he was ready for bed.

#

Birgil awoke with a tremendous phantom kick. His head pounded, mouth like cotton, and legs Charley-horsed. Stomach cramped, threatening to expel bile, as he tried to sit up, but he was stopped short. Couldn't move -something holding him down. Arms and legs bound.

"What the fu--" The statement was cut off by a callused hand clamping over Birgil's mouth. He saw the figure over the bed. Although dim, the nightlight showed the face of a bare-chested younger man with spiky red hair.

Doxey struggled against the straps. Too tight, it was no use.

"Shut up, Birgil," commanded the figure. Doxey focused on the face – slim, beardless. He couldn't have been older than twenty five. His left hand wiped away a milk mustache. "I'm going to enjoy watching you squirm..."

As the hand pulled away, Birgil tried to speak but an odorous ether-soaked rag filled his mouth. A whisper in his ear, "Eram Quod Es, Eris Quod Sum. I was what you are, you will be what I am."

The world went black.

CHAPTER 8

AETERNUM VALE:

Farewell Forever

Birgil came to, again, immobilized. Hands secured behind his back. Hemp rope itchy around his neck. Standing on a wobbly plastic crate, he wondered if the thing could hold his weight for long.

He was at Hell's Bridge. Firelight illuminated partially-cloaked figures dancing around him as if he were a Maypole. Latin chanting filled his ears.

"It's awake," spoke the spiky haired youth.

"Where am I?" Birgil asked, vision hazy.

"You know where you are," the devilish kid said, finger in Birgil's face. His voice betrayed a possible speech impediment. "And you know *why* you're here. This is hallowed ground. *His* soul is bound to the soil."

"Who're you?"

"*Ich bin* Liam Kaltenbrunner," Spiky Hair said, pulling a straight razor from his pocket. Doxey realized it wasn't a speech impediment, but rather a foreign accent. Watered down, second-generation German. With the razor, Liam cut away Birgil's shirt, exposing a round, pale belly.

"Kaltenbrunner? Son of Hans?"

"Hans was *mein* uncle," Liam explained, blade poised above belly button. "He showed me the way." The blade sliced into Birgil's gut. Surface cuts, not too deep. Just enough for a good bloodletting.

"AAAHHH," Doxey screamed, blade separating flabby flesh. Eyes darted downward, he saw what Liam was carving: a Hangman.

"FREEZE!" a voice called from above. Detective Brazo, with a double-handed grip on his service revolver, aimed at Liam. "Drop the blade!"

Liam slowly raised his hands, dropping the blade to the ground.

"Hands on your head," Brazo said, approaching.

Wearing a grin, the spiky-haired Liam appeared a demented clown. Hands behind his head, he stepped away from Birgil.

"Thank God, Detective," uttered Birgil, breathless.

"Thank God for attentive neighbors," Brazo said. "Always got their eyes peeled for trespassers."

Without taking his eyes off his targets, Brazo cut the zip tie from Doxey's wrists. Hands freed, Birgil slipped out of the noose, hopping down from the milk crate. He rubbed tender wrists.

"Thanks," he whispered to Brazo.

POP! Birgil's face was splattered with blood and brain matter. Brazo, the front of his face now a shredded pulp, sank to his knees, then dropped to the dirt.

Behind him, a robed busty blonde, smoking pistol in hand. The nurse from Golden Acres. Birgil noticed she held *his* gun.

Liam removed Brazo's pistol, still clutched by dead fingers. "I normally hang *schweine*. For you, I'll make an exception." Smiling, he lined up his shot, squeezing the trigger.

Birgil dove in front of the busty nurse, just as Liam's gun fired. Missing the top of his skull, the bullet bore through the nurse's shoulder, causing the involuntary squeeze of her own trigger finger. The round from Birgil's handgun struck the cult leader in the abdomen, knocking him backward.

Birgil recovered his gun at the feet of the bleeding

nurse. She howled in pain, clutching the wounded shoulder. He noticed Liam squirming in the mud, and kicked Brazo's revolver out of reach. "No you don't!"

Doxey grabbed the second pistol. Whirling around, he waved the guns in an arc. The cultists stepped back. Their dark magic couldn't stop bullets. He'd had enough, and on impulse, stomped Liam's gut wound.

"You're all under citizen's arrest," Doxey announced, soliciting giggles from the unmoving cultists. He knew he couldn't physically restrain each one until help arrived – he wondered what to do.

"I need an ambulance," the busty nurse cried.

"Shut up," growled Liam, blood pouring between his fingers. He tried to continue, but choked on his words.

Tucking the revolver under his belt, Doxey dug in his pocket. He found the emergency cell. Eyes flicked downward, thumb hit the "call" button when he felt the fiery stab of pain shoot through his shoulder.

He spun on his heel. There stood Liam Kaltenbrunner, lower torso, legs drenched in blood. Crimson dripped from a double-sided ceremonial dagger.

"You son of a bitch," Doxey muttered through gritted teeth. He trained the gun on Liam, but the spiky haired leader swiftly slashed his enemy's hand. The blade cut deep, severing muscle, tendon, and arteries. "Shit," Birgil swore, dropping the gun.

Crazy-eyed Liam rushed his adversary, dagger swiping the air. Birgil held out his uninjured hand, trying to fend off the attack. Wrist and fingers were cut to ribbons, the sharp edge shredding with every contact. The head cultist was impervious to his injuries.

A crooked root jutting out from the soil caught Doxey's foot as a stumbled backwards. He landed flat on his ass, looking up as robed figures surrounded him. They drew their own blades.

"Please," Doxey begged. Dozens of pricks, pokes, and stabs opened his flesh, giving his blood new openings from which to seep. He understood these would be his last moments. Then he remembered – Brazo's gun tucked under his belt.

Kaltenbrunner smiled, exposing blood-stained teeth. He straddled Doxey's legs, holding the dagger high above his head.

"Hush. Don't cry. For *him*, you shall die..."

"FOR *HIM*!!" "FOR *HIM*!!!" echoed the Faithful.

Doxey pulled the revolver, pointed, and squeezed the trigger. One cultist down. Another fell to the ground, silent – not screaming like the first one. Fatal head wound. Firing

again, a fleeing Faithful fell at an odd angle, knee shattered.
A round to the spine silenced the screaming.

Red hair over the sights, Doxey discharged a final
round.

Uninjured cultists fled, melting away into the darkness.
The dead or dying were all that remained.

Liam was sprawled on his back, bleeding from the
second bullet in the chest.

Struggling to his feet, Doxey felt no sympathy. This evil
little demon-lover slaughtered local kids (and animals) for
the simple reason he, and a twisted dead uncle, admired the
legend of a child killer.

"Fuck you," Birgil said. Liam's head rolled to the side,
whites of his eyes exposed. Shot lined up, Doxey pulled the
trigger.

Nothing. Out of bullets. Eyes searching the ground, he
saw the dagger.

Flashing blue and red lights appeared in the distance.
Doxey's emergency call had gone through. The cavalry en
route.

Birgil took a knee next to his enemy, raised the dagger,
still slick with his own blood. His hand quivered, readying to
plunge the knife deep into the dark heart.

Liam's eyes fluttered. "Do it," he whispered. "End it..."

"THERE HE IS," shouted a voice from above. Sirens screamed, car doors slamming.

"THERE'S THE HANGMAN! HE'S ABOUT TO KILL ANOTHER KID!!"

"HANDS UP!!"

"DROP THE WEAPON!!"

Ears ringing, high on adrenaline, Doxey didn't detect the presence of the police. All he saw was the face of evil in front of him... and his chance to kill it.

Dozens of pistols and shotguns fired their loads into Birgil Doxey's significant frame. Blown sideways, the big man rolled away, the dagger falling to his side. On his back, he stared at the moon.

The heart gave a final thump and then... failed.

"Got the son of a bitch!" one of the triumphant policeman shouted.

Another approached Liam, bending down to look at his face. "Don't worry, son," the policeman reassured. "Ambulances are on the way. You're going to be okay. Hang in there."

"Detective Brazo's dead," remarked another cop mournfully, standing over his fallen colleague.

Liam's bloody hand shot out, startling the policeman. He grasped the cop's hairy hand, squeezed. The cop mistook the gesture as one of a scared kid who wanted someone to hold his hand. Removing his service cap, the officer looked around at the carnage. Blood, odd ceremonial items scattered around... empty noose swinging in the wind.

"Who was he? Who did this to you, son?" The cop cupped his other hand over Liam's, trying comfort him.

"I think they call him the 'Hangman...'"

"Son of a bitch," swore a deputy. "That's Birgil Doxey."

"You mean the Bigfoot Hunter? I knew that guy was weird... but *this* weird?"

After the ambulance finally arrived, Liam was loaded into the back. He cracked a vicious smile as the doors closed.

"Cursum Perficio." My journey is over.

#

Hours later, after the body of Birgil Doxey was zipped in a bag and taken away, and the crime scene secured, one of the remaining detectives glanced around the location. His eyes locked on the rusted iron footbridge over the water.

"Damn this place," the cop said, shaking his head.

Walking away, the policeman didn't see the reflected image in the water. The grey, bearded, transparent face lined

65

with wrinkles.

Elias Friske smiled.

THE END

ABOUT THE AUTHOR

Russell Slater is a writer from western Michigan. His work has been published in the (Wayland) *Penasee Globe, Allegan County News,* Engraver's Journal, Flavor 616 Magazine, and the Volunteer: Civil Air Patrol Magazine. He lives in a rural community with his wife and son.

Contact the author:
Russell@peninsulampublishing.com

Peninsulam Publishing

www.peninsulampublishing.com

Return to Strange Home

By Peter Welmerink

$6.99 (Now available)

Michigan 2065. Nobody home, and Mother Nature has reclaimed the land… for the most part.

After ten long years, Captain Paul Wells returns from deep space. He's ready to be home, along the sand-swept shores of Lake Michigan. However, his home is not how he left it.

The security system wants to fry him in his boots. Someone has infiltrated his place, and is powerful enough to instantly put him six feet under. And there are new entities patrolling the land, alerted to his homecoming, who are intent on making it his last.

Determined to reclaim his dwelling, Wells doesn't plan to be a strange in this strange home for long.

<u>Acipenser:</u>

<u>Green Lake Monster</u>

By Russell Slater

$3.99 (Now available)

Residents of a small West Michigan town must contend with giant genetically mutated creatures who emerge from the depths of a local lake to wreck havoc over a 4th of July weekend.

West Michigan Rising

By Russell Slater

$9.99 (Now available)

Set in the fictional nation of the Great Lakes Commonwealth,
citizens of West Michigan struggle for their right to possess
firearms against an overreaching and tyrannical central government.